Engineer Ari and the
Rosh Hashanah Ride

For my sister, Kim, who shares her love of reading with young children–D.B.C

For my grandmother, Hannah, who passed on her creative genes to me. –S.K.

Special thanks to Chen Melling at the Israel Railway Museum in Haifa
for her generous help with research and questions.

Text copyright © 2008 by Deborah Bodin Cohen
Illustrations © 2008 Lerner Publishing Group, Inc.
Photo p.32 by Garabad Krikorian, Armenian Patriarchate Collection

KAR-BEN PUBLISHING
A division of Lerner Publishing Group, Inc.
241 First Avenue North
Minneapolis, MN 55401 U.S.A.
1-800-4KARBEN

Website address: www.karben.com

Library of Congress Cataloging-in-Publication Data

Cohen, Deborah Bodin, 1968–
   Engineer Ari and the Rosh Hashanah ride / by Deborah Bodin
Cohen ; illustrated by Shahar Kober.
      p.   cm.
   Summary: Israel's first train chugs from Jaffa to Jerusalem on
Rosh Hashanah.
    ISBN 978–0–8225–8648–7 (lib. bdg. : alk. paper)
   [1. Railroad trains—Fiction. 2. Rosh ha-Shanah—Fiction.] I. Kober,
Shahar, ill. II. Title.
   PZ7.C6623En 2008
   [E—dc22   2007043123

Manufactured in the United States of America
4 – DP – 3/9/12

GLOSSARY

Challah: egg bread eaten on Sabbath and Jewish holidays

Rosh Hashanah: Jewish New Year

Shanah Tovah: Happy New Year

Shofar: ram's horn blown on Rosh Hashanah to usher in new year

Teshuvah: literally "turning around"; repentance

Yom Kippur: Day of Atonement

Engineer Ari
and the
Rosh Hashanah Ride

By Deborah Bodin Cohen
illustrations by Shahar Kober

KAR-BEN
PUBLISHING

Engineer Ari walked proudly into the railway station in the port city of Jaffa. The year was 1892. The workers had finished the tracks just in time for Rosh Hashanah.

"A new year, a new railway," thought Engineer Ari, "and I've been chosen to drive the first train from Jaffa to Jerusalem."

He patted the train's boiler.

"Are you ready?" he asked. "You and I are going to deliver Rosh Hashanah treats to the children in Jerusalem."

Ari's engineer friends Jessie and Nathaniel stood nearby. "Look at the crowds who came to see me off," Ari boasted to them.

Nathaniel sulked because he hadn't been chosen.

Jessie grumbled, "Ari thinks he is so important."

"We can't all be first," Ari bragged. He told himself not to worry about Jessie and Nathaniel.

Engineer Ari climbed into the train's cab.
He tugged the whistle cord.

"Toot, Toot!"

The switchman gave the signal. The crowd
cheered and clapped.

Engineer Ari pulled back the throttle and the
train steamed out of the station.

He forgot to say good-bye to Jessie and Nathaniel.

The train **CHUG-a-LUGGED** past cypress trees and orange groves. Children waved as the train went by.

The train hissed slowly into the first station.
A girl hurried out of the crowd, carrying a basket.
   "Please bring these apples to Jerusalem for a
sweet new year," she said. "My uncle grew them
in his orchard."
   Engineer Ari took a juicy bite out of a shiny,
green apple.
   The color reminded him of Jessie.
   Jessie's train engine was bright green.
   Ari wondered if Jessie was still angry.

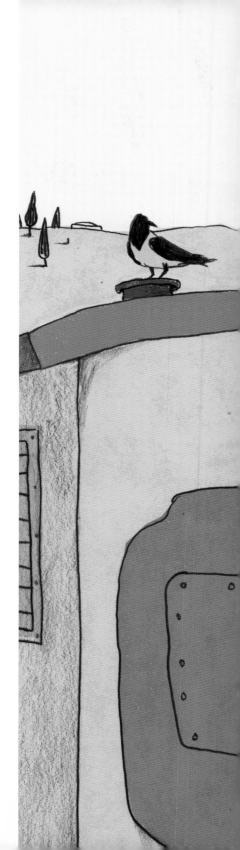

"Shanah Tovah, Happy New Year!" called Engineer Ari, steaming out of the station. He tugged the whistle cord.

"Toot, Toot!"

The train CHUG-a-LUGGED past palm trees and prickly pear cactus. A beekeeper looked up from her honeycombs to wave.

At the next station, a boy lifted a crate filled with jars and brought it to the platform.

"Are you going to Jerusalem?" he asked, holding up a jar.

"Please take my mother's honey with you so the children of Jerusalem can dip apples in honey on Rosh Hashanah."

Engineer Ari smiled at the thought of the sweet, sticky honey.

But the golden color reminded him of Nathaniel.

Nathaniel's train engine was sunny yellow.

Ari worried that he had hurt Nathaniel's feelings.

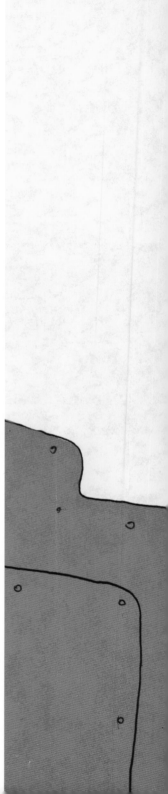

"Shanah Tovah, Happy New Year!" called Engineer Ari, steaming out of the station. He tugged the whistle cord.

"Toot, Toot!"

The train CHUG-A-LUGGED toward gray foothills.
Farmers waved from their wheat fields.

At the next station, a baker and his son hurried out of the crowd carrying large sacks. The sweet smell of fresh bread filled the air.

"What smells so good?" asked Engineer Ari.

"My son and I have baked loaves of round challah," said the baker. "Please bring them to Jerusalem for Rosh Hashanah."

Engineer Ari thought about Jessie again.

She loved the smell of fresh bread.

Ari wished he had not bragged to his friends.

The train CHUG-a-LUGGED into a narrow canyon and began to climb slowly as the tracks curved through steep hills. A shepherd tended his flock. One ram had long, curled horns. The ram looked up and let out a loud "baa."

At the next station, a boy carrying a large basket on his head walked toward the tracks.

He took a shofar out of the basket and blew a strong, deep note. "My family makes these shofars from rams' horns. Please bring them to Jerusalem so people can announce the New Year."

Engineer Ari thought about Nathaniel.

If Nathaniel had heard the shofar, he would have pulled his train's whistle cord to make the same sounds.

He wondered how he could apologize to his friends.

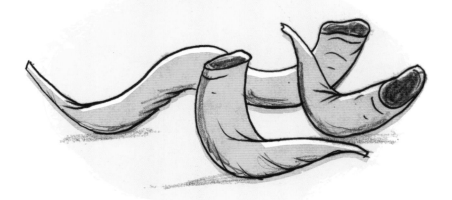

"Shanah Tovah, Happy New Year!" called Engineer Ari, steaming out of the station. He tugged the whistle cord.

"Toot, Toot!"

The train **CHUG-a-LUGGED** higher and higher, past olive groves and underground springs. Finally, it reached a plateau.

"I can see the Jordan River from here," said Engineer Ari with excitement. He added sadly, "I wish Nathaniel and Jessie were here, too."

Before he knew it, the great walled city of Jerusalem appeared in the distance. Engineer Ari pulled into the station. The train hissed to a stop. A crowd of people cheered.

Children surrounded the train, climbing into the caboose and cab. They lifted out the Rosh Hashanah treats.

Engineer Ari hardly noticed. He was thinking about his friends.

"I hurt Jessie and Nathaniel's feelings when I bragged," he thought. "On Rosh Hashanah and Yom Kippur, we apologize for our mistakes. We do *teshuvah*. Teshuvah means turning ourselves around and promising to do better."

Engineer Ari gathered an apple, a jar of honey, a challah, and a shofar for each of his friends.

He patted the train's boiler again and said, "I need to turn you around so we can steam back to Jaffa. I want to find Jessie and Nathaniel and say I am sorry. I want to do teshuvah."

"Shanah Tovah, Happy New Year!" called Engineer Ari, steaming out of the station. He tugged the whistle cord.

"Toot, Toot!"

Author's Note

On August 27, 1892, the first train steamed into Jerusalem from Jaffa, carrying passengers and cargo. A month later, during the High Holidays, the railway officially opened. The train shortened the trip between the Mediterranean coast and Jerusalem from 3 days to 3½ hours. Eliezer Ben-Yehuda, the father of modern Hebrew, who lived in Jerusalem at the time, coined the word *rakevet* (train) from the Biblical word for "chariot."

The railway began as a modest operation with three trains built by the Baldwin Locomotive

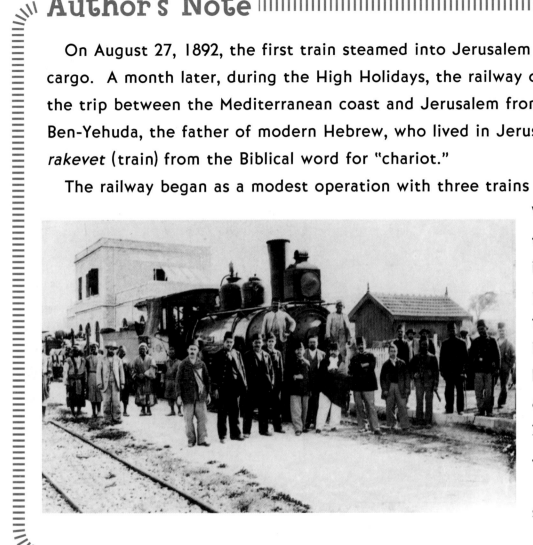

Works of Philadelphia. It was rumored that the trains were originally intended for the first Panama Canal project. When this project failed, the trains were shipped to Jaffa instead. The railway was 55 miles long, made 6 stops between Jaffa and Jerusalem, and rose nearly 2500 feet as it curved through the Judean mountains.

Parts of this historic scenic railway still operate today.